A Big Black Castle with Silver Space Ships

By Thomas Zoltan Ban

Order this book online at www.trafford.com
or email orders@trafford.com

Most Trafford titles are also available at major online book retailers.

Printed in Victoria, BC, Canada.

ISBN: 978-1-4269-2229-9

*Our mission is to efficiently provide the world's finest, most
comprehensive book publishing service, enabling every author to
experience success. To find out how to publish your book, your way, and
have it available worldwide, visit us online at www.trafford.com*

Trafford rev. 11/04/09

 www.trafford.com

North America & international
toll-free: 1 888 232 4444 (USA & Canada)
phone: 250 383 6864 ♦ fax: 812 355 4082

Do you want to evolve to the next stage in human development?

Then read this book!

With a wry wit like that of Oscar Wilde, a choppy style like that of Kurt Vonnegut, and a blatant candor like that of Hugh Hefner, this book reveals how reality is nothing more than a big mathematical chemical reaction of principles, perfections, Identities, and MAGIC!!!

In this, part collection of science fiction short stories, part autobiography of a madman, the author delves into concepts dealing with hell safety, pathos, friendliness, love, magic, knowledge and variety. With an inimicable style, he excites the senses and satisfies the desire for scintillating fascination and the hope for a better future, with love, charity, peace, and above all, friendliness reigning supreme.

This book is dedicated to my brother Ed, for always telling me to "Get a job"

Contents

Introduction

Hi, my name's Tom. I'm not really supposed to be here tonight because I'm really a very serious person. Are there any Eskimos in the audience tonight? No? Well, I'm not going to tell that joke tonight anyway because man are those Eskimos ever tough! I mean they live in snow forts in the Arctic and carry harpoons and eat raw seal meat all day long.

Even the Polar bears are afraid of them. Has anyone ever heard of a Polar bear eating an Eskimo? If they did, all of the Eskimos would be gone by now. After all, the Eskimos have been in their winter wasteland ever since the Chinese migrated to North America across the land bridge between Russia and Alaska, so long ago.

I'll bet you didn't know that all humans are no further apart than 50th cousin. It's true!...

Back when dinosaurs were becoming extinct, tiny lizards evolved into mice, who evolved into squirrels, who evolved into lemurs, who evolved into monkeys, who evolved into baboons, who evolved into chimps, who evolved into gorillas, who evolved into Neanderthal men, who evolved into Cro-Magnon men, who evolved into Ethiopian Negroes, who evolved into Egyptians, who evolved into East Indians, who evolved into Arabs, who evolved into Jews, who evolved into Europeans, who evolved into Ukrainians, who evolved into Russians, who evolved into Chinese, who evolved into Eskimos, who evolved into North American Indians, who evolved into Mayans, Aztecs, and Incas, who evolved into life's highest form…South American cocaine traffickers.

Actually, this book is about my preoccupation with the concept of "Hell" and how friendliness and variety may save us from it.

Orange juice on my mudflat

I dreamt I was in a desert, made of cracked mud…

It was a scene to be repeated forever, without blossom or bud.

In my case I am wandering under the hot sun, looking for all the world like a dilapidated moose…When all of a sudden, in a scene to be repeated forever, I stumble across a puddle of orange juice.

Now some men may have palaces, to break the monotony of hell; And some men may have starlet fat, but let me tell…Nothing could feel as good as orange juice on my mudflat!

Sunrise in Hell.

Professor Johnathan Reynolds squinted through the eyepiece of the main telescope of the Hubble Observatory. He couldn't believe what he saw. It looked like an S.S.T.- shaped U.F.O. approaching Earth at a ridiculous speed.

He got on the phone to General Frank Packhurst of the local military installation, and told him about it. Prof. Reynolds told the General that it looked like the spaceship was going to land in the Mojave Desert.

Packhurst organized a liaison party of troops to meet the ship where it landed. When the troops finally found the ship, it was parked, glowing an iridescent, purplish

color. It was an S.S.T. shape alright, in fact, it was an exact replica of a Concord S.S.T., although it was a little bit bigger.

The troops positioned themselves roughly 100 yards from the ship's nose.

Suddenly a hatch opened and a narrow ramp came out of it. The troops held their breaths, and presently nine "human beings" came out of the hatch and proceeded down the ramp.

The alien humans approached the troops. The aliens were all dressed in black, and they were all wearing dark sunglasses. One of them was a stunning looking female.

When the aliens reached the commander of the troops, the lead alien spoke...

"We are from the planet Excaliber. Please take us to the leader of your planet, as we have business to conduct with him."

The commander ushered the aliens into a truck, and drove them to the nearest military base. A Lear jet was waiting for them, there.

The aliens were flown to Washington D.C.,... to the White House, in particular.

In the Oval Office, President Bush was waiting impatiently, for them. He was flanked by T.V. crews and news reporters.

The aliens were given seats in front of the President's desk.

"Now, What can I do for you people?" asked Mr. Bush.

The aliens, as one, all took off their sunglasses. President Bush and everyone else in the room, were all shocked to see that the aliens' eyes all looked like snake eyes, with evil looking slits for pupils, instead of round pupils.

The lead alien spoke…"My name is Rom. We are people whose basic possibility characteristics are mainly hell powers, making us hell power people.

We come from a planet where an abundant nature abounds, with the nine of us being the only predators on the planet. We are carnivorous and only hunt and eat bunnies, which we catch with weapons supplied to us by godly machines. These machines also supply us with everything else we need.

Our basic possibility hell powers chemical reactionally let us know that it was required of us to send our bunny prey to hell, or our hell powers would turn on us instead. They supplied us with "hell slivers" to inject into the bunnies.

We were afraid of retaliation, so we injected the hell slivers into some bunnies.

Not long afterwards, our brains were invaded by telepathic messages from the central God-machine Identity herself. She is in charge of all of the sensations, creation, destruction, and evolution arrangement in the corporeal universe.

The God-machine Identity told us that she was furious with us for almost sending her bunnies to hell, which she just barely averted. She said she was going to send us to hell instead, because she was so angry with us.

We begged and begged with her not to do it. We said we were only scared of our hell-powers sending us to hell, if we didn't do what they wanted.

The God-machine Identity was firm in her decision.

The female among us hell-power people had an idea. She was the most sexually attractive female in existence at the time, and she told the God Identity, that she would give the God the best sex ever, if the God would not send them to hell.

The God Identity liked the idea, and when it was all over, the God Identity said she was sending all nine of us to half safety, half pain, forever, because she was still somewhat angry with us.

We begged her to send us to be among the luckiest heaven recipients, so that wecould feed off of their sanity.

She sent us to you, the ultimate classic civilization; with all of you going to heaven too. That is why we are here. Can we stay?"

President Bush thought about how it was wrong to anger the God-machine Identity. He thought about how his faith in the Bible was shattered. He thought about the hell-power people's evil looking eyes. He thought and thought. Finally he sighed and said " You may stay."

The End

Ring of Gold

John winced. He couldn't understand the language, but he knew his joyride through Nepal and India was over. After all, this uniformed peasant in front of him was now pointing a gun at him. John sighed. Rather than get shot for being uncooperative, he reached into the crotch of his pants and retrieved the 2 pounds of hashish in his money belt, and handed it to the uniformed clown waving a gun.

Earth in the year 2050 was much like any civilization. Wars broke out, the saints would end them, then everyone was prosperous, then came the renaissance of the mind, then decadence, then rebellion, then poverty, then war again. One thing different about the year 2050 was the fact that for the first time in man's history, man was visited by superior extraterrestrial beings.

These creatures had vast nuclear power deposits, entire planets of uranium, which fueled their adventures. Their favorite pastime was to travel through space in search of greater riches, and also for amusement, Their spacecraft were mostly saucer-shaped disks with tele-port-capability. Teleport was accomplished by blowing up their ships and sending the electron-sized particles on light beams much more powerful than laser beams. Traveling at the speed of light, the ship particles soon arrive at any destination in the galaxy, where a 3-D grid of computer-assisted electromagnets rebuild the ship and it's crew from a distance (at one time this alien civ-ilization had posted, around the galaxy, large electro-magnets [powered by uranium planets], with which to attract coded spacecraft fragments).

The aliens had been using this system for so long that, through the generations, they had evolved the power to change their forms at will. Their basic shape looked like octopuses devouring men headfirst (two legs and waist high, octopus arms and snail heads). The aliens called themselves the Arronx, They quickly learned English and explained themselves to the news reporters…

"We are cannibals, but we never eat flesh of others than our own race. We have no leaders or caste system because of this. Each one of us is fully honorable, with power struggles seeming an insult to each worthy one of us. The reason why we are here is to retrieve a sacred religious icon, which was lost here the last time we were here. It is a teleport device, fashioned in the form of an east-Indian gold and diamond bracelet. It could be anywhere on the planet."

John whistled. "Boy, I'll bet there's a reward by the U.N. for the bracelet!" He was watching the news on T.V. in his cell in prison. "If I could get my hands on that bracelet, I'd be on easy street," John said. All of a sudden, out of one of the corners of the communal jail-cell, arose a wavering voice; "I will lead you to the bracelet, for a price!"

John squinted in the dark, and barely made out an old and crumpled form in the twilight of life. "How?" asked John. "Two things, you must do," replied the old man. "First you must get me out of jail, and back to my station as Prince of Calcutta; and the second thing you must do, to have your bidding, is to marry my deformed daughter. You see, she is so homely looking, that I can't seem to find her a husband; and she is getting so depressed that it breaks my heart to see her."

John said, "I'll get you out of here or my name isn't John Johnson!" John had already been thinking about how he would get out of jail. He had written, in code, a letter to his brother in Colorado, and in the letter he had asked his brother to send the family robot to save him. In the ancient Hindi jail, with it's dirt floor, the robot would have no trouble tunneling in, and then take them to a stolen airplane and out of the country.

Two days after John made the deal with the old prince, the robot came through the floor. The seven occupants of the jail couldn't all fit into the airplane, so two were left behind to fall prey to the mercy of the uniformed-ones.

Back in the States, the foreign embassy to the United States from India quickly cleared up the matter with Indian authorities. Apparently the Prince had been mistaken for a common criminal, and the King of India presented a full pardon and an apology to him.

John was anxious to get the bracelet, so he asked the Prince about it, the morning after the pardon was granted. So the two of them flew back to India, to the Taj Mahal in particular. It was here that the Prince pointed to a bracelet on a golden statue of Shiva dancing to create the universe. John was shook up. How was he to steal the bracelet from the well-guarded Taj Mahal? "Why don't you try teleporting out of here, using the bracelet's powers?" asked the Prince. John thought it was a splendid idea, He retrieved the bracelet from the statue, and began fiddling with the decorations on it.

One of the diamonds on the bracelet was a power switch, which turned on the teleport machinations, and before he knew it, John exploded into electrons and lost consciousness. A few moments later he found himself lying on a metal table, in what looked like a futuristic operating room, in some technologically crazed hospital.

John soon found out that he had accidentally teleported himself to a receptor table on the home planet of the alien visitors. An alien nurse, who looked like a cross between a butterfly and a praying mantis, discovered him. She had a mantis body, butterfly wings and head.

John explained himself to the nurse, and she took him and the bracelet to a government office (run by volunteers). The president of the office quickly ate her and then turned to John. "You may have any gift you desire", said the alienbureaucrat. "What have you got?" asked John. "We have spacecraft, exotic virtual reality vacations, real estate on uranium planets, star core chunks to put on your mantle piece, excursions to heaven…" "Wait!" said John, "what was that last one?" "Excursions to heaven, by the sacred power crystals. We can actually send you to heaven, and your friends too, by the magic of the power crystals. I'm personally in a heaven myself, right as we speak," said the diplomat.

"Wow! That's for me!" shouted John. "Can you transcend the entire human race to heaven too?" "Yes, we can… in fact, we recommend such an action!" answered the alien. "Well, let's get started, then," said John. The alien used the bracelet to teleport the two of them to the alien planet's core, which was hollow; and in the very centre of the planet, floated the power crystals, shining too brightly to be gazed upon.

"Before you go to heaven, you must be educated as to the perfect laws, as is our religious custom", said the alien diplomat (whose name was "Hore")." First of all, there is no infinite variety of phenomenon possible. There are only the basic possibilities (or perfect laws) repeated over and over again, throughout eternity.

These possibilities are:

1. Nothingness
1. Creation 2. Destruction
1. Power 2. Density 3. Motion
1. Combinations 2. Merger-fades 3. Infiniteness 4. Finiteness
1. Pain 2. Pleasure 3. Blandness 4. Unconsciousness 5. Consciousness
1. Point 2. Line 3. Curve 4. Plane 5. Space 6. Time
1. Accidentalness 2. Impossibilities 3. Possibilityness 4. Chaos 5. Logic
6. Numbers 7. Official facts (Like a person's soul is basically made of)
1. Burning 2. Hot 3. Warm 4. Luke 5. Tepid 6. Cool 7. Cold 8. Freezing
1. Black 2. Brown 3. Red 4. Orange 5. Yellow 6. Green 7. Blue 8. Violet
9. White
1. Scents 2. Flavors 3. Sounds and other tactile sensations 4. Concept
meanings (if, how, why, humour, culture, entertainment, stories, adventures,
syncopation, volition, goodnesses, happiness, love, comfort, beauty, thrills,
etc.) 5. Evolution 6. Truth knowledge 7. Desire and satisfaction 8. Moods
9. Realityness 10. Magic (Caused by conflicting logics or existing just as is,
like colors, pleasure, consciousness, and people have a lot of).

Permutations of the previous exist, as do people themselves (a pure magic).Nothing else exists but these laws, except for the fact that time had to have a beginning. Just as the present will never be forever in the future, it simply can't have actually been in the eternal past."

"Gotcha", said John. "Now, can we humans go to heaven?" "Yes", said Hore, "now you may." All of a sudden something felt different to John. He was no longer afraid. He felt an incredible weight lifted from his chest…The weight of a life-long fear of death, injury, and pain… and he found this fear replaced by an incredible enthusiasm. Then the pleasure started, and John did what most creatures did when they entered heaven, he began to laugh with joy and cry with relief!

John thanked the alien official and asked to be excused to return to Earth, as he had a bride waiting for him back on Earth. Back on Earth, it was a regular party scene. People were running amok in the streets, rejoicing and praising John's name (as the aliens had informed Earth of these latest developments). When John got to see his bride for the first time, her mutant face looked like the face of an angel, as seen under the influence of heaven.

Human beings lived happily forever and ever, mutating and evolving at will, under the beautiful blanket of heaven, never to feel pain again.

The End

Friendliness is still king

Once there was a very fat frog, named Theodore. He ate like a pig all of the time. He had a coyote pup friend named Paco. Theodore and Paco were in cahoots. They would go down to bars together, and shoot women.

One woman, named Angelina, with the most beautiful breasts in eternity, was in a bar one night. She saw Paco and Theodore enter. As the two animals started shooting all of the women in the bar, Angelina quickly hid behind a shower curtain, in the washroom.

Behind the shower curtain, Angelina started to cry. Then she took her clothes off, and stepped out on the floor to meet her fate. As soon as she reached the barroom floor, Paco and Theodore shot her with their Colt pistols, through the head and heart. Angelina crumpled over into a lifeless heap.

Paco said "Let's get out of here." Theodore said "I hear the Brain Police coming, let's split!" They both took off into the night. They went to a crack dealer and picked up some crack cocaine. They took it to their hideaway. In their mountain top house, they smoked their faces off. Paco turned to Theodore and said, "Let's take the space saucer to the moon tonight." Theodore said "Okay, maybe we can go crater baby hunting." "Yeah!" said Paco.

The two cohorts got into their flying saucer. They turned on the ignition burners. Then they revved the acceleration switch. Paco pressed the take-off button and they began rising. Theodore monkeyed the computer panel and plotted their course for The Sea of Tranquility, Luna, U.S.A. Then he pressed the engage switch. Within moments they were waking up, after the deceleration wore off. Then they were damping down on the crunchy moon's surface. They put on their breathing apparatus, and then they popped the hatch.

By radio, Paco said "Hey, I see some Lunar sea snakes over there! Let's go see if we can ray some of them." The two errant buddies hurried over to where the glistening serpents were sliding through the dust. They managed to melt one of them, before the snakes disappeared.

Suddenly Paco and Theodore fell through a hole in the ground, which was hidden by a black shadow. They found themselves in a big cavern under the lunar surface. After dusting themselves off, they lit a lamp and looked around themselves. They saw a tunnel ahead of them, which looked like it was lined with crystals.

Suddenly a bat-like ghoul, in a laboratory smock, appeared out of a shadow of a crevice. He was surprised to see Paco and Theodore, and he fumbled for a weapon. Paco drew first, and melted the bat. Then the two animals investigated the crevice from which the bat had entered. They found a crystal tunnel, which they could barely fit into. The tunnel was square in shape, and very long. It disappeared into the distance. Paco and Theodore crawled for miles and miles, always going straight. Finally they saw a glow at the end of the tunnel. It was a purplish glow. They reached the end of the tunnel, and found themselves in a forest-filled cavern. It was maybe a hundred miles across.

The two guys wandered amongst the trees, occasionally stopping to shoot a bird, or eat wonkleberries. There were bird-headed monkeys everywhere. They reached a gingerbread house, with a candy roof. They knocked on the door. A wolf in sheep's clothing answered. "YES?!?" asked the wolf. Paco said "We're hungry." "Come in," said the wolf. The two entered the house. It was a plain house, with gyproc walls and antique furniture. It was immaculately maintained by outward appearances, but there was a faint scent of moldy socks in the air. "Sit down," said the wolf, as he motioned to the table and chairs. Then the wolf puttered about the kitchen alcove, as he rustled up some grub. While the three animals ate, they talked. "Where are you going?" asked the wolf. "No where," said Paco. "By the way, what is this place?' asked Theodore.

"This is the cavern of the God-machine," said the wolf. "God-machine?" asked Paco. "Yes," said the wolf, "It's the perfection-machine in charge of arranging the whole corporeal universe into a particular order."

Suddenly the three animals heard a scraping and crunching sound. The wolf jumped up and looked out the window. "Oh no!" shrieked the wolf. "It's a tribe of rabid skunks, and they're eating my house!" Some holes in the walls began appearing, and skunks began popping in. Paco and Theodore began raying skunks. The melted skunks blocked up the holes, but more holes began appearing. Finally Paco yelled, "Make for the door, before the roof caves in!" They opened the door and started raying a pathway through the skunk horde. When they were finally out of the fracas, they breathed a sigh of relief.

"What now?" asked Paco. "Well, my home is destroyed," said the wolf. "The only thing left to do, is to find the God-machine and get my home replaced." "Maybe we can send ourselves to heaven in the process," drooled Theodore, "just think of all the girls we could have our heavens in the form of!"

The three wandered for miles through the forest. Eventually they began to notice a powerful, booming sort of high-pitched, screaming, whining sound. They made towards the noise. They finally entered a clearing where they could see a jumbo jet airline terminal. The noise was completely deafening by then, and totally shattered their senses to moldy crisp-dust.

They wandered over to one of the jets. There didn't seem to be anyone around, so they went up the gangplank and entered the aircraft. Inside, a robot stewardess greeted them and showed them to their seats. The noise was unbearable. As soon as the aircraft took off, the noise stopped.

Paco asked the stewardess where they were going. "To the God-machine!" answered the stewardess. "It is your destiny to turn it on. You are the first to meet the entry requirements. Here are your clearance cards." She handed them three metallic plastic-like cards, which glowed a heavenly white color. When the jet landed, the three animals found themselves in a big hanger, all covered in computers. It was such a big hanger, that, the massive jumbo jet was dwarfed by it.

Some monkeys approached Paco and Theodore and the wolf. They checked the clearance cards, and said, "You must be central programmers. Please come with us." The monkeys led them to a side-room. In the room there was a glowing console with three buttons. The buttons were made of diamonds.

The monkeys said, "The first button sends everyone to hell. The second button sends everyone to a sexless heaven. The third button gives all of us here in the compound, including yourselves, the best sex imaginably possible, and sends us to heaven, and everyone else to hell. We want you to push the third button, after you insert your clearance cards.

The three inserted their cards. Paco was elected to press the button. With Theodore and the wolf and the monkeys watching him, Paco thought of all of the creatures he had slaughtered, in his hedonist life. He thought of all the poor souls who would go to hell, to give him heavenly sex. A tear trickled down his cheek. Then, before anyone could stop him, he quickly pressed the second button, and sent everyone to a sexless heaven.

The monkeys howled. Theodore asked, "What did you do that for, Paco?" Paco answered, "I guess friendliness is still king."

The End

The Enchanted Castle

Once, long ago and not too far from here, there lived a very friendly king. His name was King James, and he lived in a big, black castle, on the top of the highest mountain in his domain. He had been looking far and wide for a wife, for a long time, and he had recently found the most beautiful woman in the world. Her name was Lady Ismerelda, and she and the king were to be married the very next day.

Deep in the dungeon of the black castle, in a secret room, there existed a tiny enchanted castle, which was only two feet high. In this castle lived a fairy princess. Her name was Elana, and she was the last of the faeries, which made her very lonely. She did , however, have an entire kingdom of insects, to keep her company. Her royal court was made up of moths and butterflies. Her royal advisors were praying mantises and grasshoppers. The royal guard was made up of wasps and bumblebees. The royal servants were ants and beetles.

The fairy princess was very beautiful, even more beautiful than Lady Ismerelda. Her hair was bright gold, her skin pale white, and her lips were a cherry red. Her clothing was made of flower petals. Elana was secretly in love with King James.

The king had asked Lady Ismerelda to live in the big black castle, until they were married. It was while an ant was in a mouse tunnel next to Lady Ismerelda's room, that the ant overheard Lady Ismerelda talking to one of King James' royal hunters, "As soon as the king and I are married, you must kill him. Then I will be ruler of this land, and you will get one-fifth of the royal treasure. Now go, and tell no one what is to pass."

The little ant hurried to the enchanted castle. When she got there, she quickly told the fairy princess Elana what she had overheard. Elana devised a plan. She had a bumblebee guard fly her to the king's dining chamber. The chamber was empty and the table was set. The fairy princess sprinkled some invisible magic shrinking powder into the king's goblet. Then she hid in the mouse tunnel leading into the room.

A little while later, the king and two guards entered. The king sat down, and the royal cooks entered, bearing trays of succulent foods and flasks of sweet wines. The cooks then left, and the king began to eat. When he took a drink of wine from the goblet with the magic powder in it, he began to feel a little ill. "Guards, go fetch the royal physician, as I feel slightly ill," said the king.

Almost immediately after the guards had left, the king stood up to clear his head. Suddenly everything started to grow. In actuality, it was the king who was shrinking. By the time he was one inch tall, the fairy princess had caught his attention. Then she beckoned him to the mouth of the mouse tunnel. She hurriedly told him of the evil

Lady Ismerelda's wicked plan to kill him. The king was overwhelmed with gratitude. He took the fairy princess in his arms, and kissed her.

The next day the king and the fairy princess were married in the enchanted castle, and they lived there happily ever after.

The Enchanted Castle
Part two

James and Elana lived happily for many months in the tiny, secret castle, with it's butterfly and moth nobility, bumblebee and wasp guards, ant and beetle servants, and grasshopper and praying mantis priests, scientists and doctors. As the months wore on, however, the king began to miss his friends and relatives, in the rest of the castle. James told Elana of his inclination to grow big again. Elana said she would arrange it with her scientists.

"But how will you, Elana, grow to join me, and meet my friends and relatives, in the grand reunion?" asked the king. Elana said, "There is a way. But it is very dangerous. On an island in the sea, lies a fire-breathing dragon, guarding the stolen 'Jewel of the Faeries'. Only with this gem may I grow to human size. If you are brave enough to steal the jewel and bring it back to me , you may have your wish. But I beg you, not to try it."

James wouldn't hear of it. He summoned a praying mantis scientist to give him some growing powder and some sleeping powder. James kissed Elana goodbye, and then he swallowed some of the growing powder. He left the secret room, and immediately he grew to his original human size. He went upstairs to his court-room, where he found that Lady Ismerelda had taken over his castle. King James immediately had her thrown into the dungeon.

All of the king's family and friends were very happy to see him again. After a homecoming banquet, in which the king told all that had transpired in the past few months, the king summoned for his pet falcon to be brought to him. The king fed the falcon some growing powder, and the falcon grew to the size of a horse. Bidding his family goodbye, the king mounted the falcon, and flew off over the balcony, headed for the sea.

The king and the falcon flew many miles over the sea, until finally the tiny island of the dragon came into view. The king approached it, and had the falcon land in a forest, at one end of the island. Then the king dismounted, and crept through the forest, until he came to a clearing. The clearing had a pond, and a hill with a cave entrance on it's side. The king poured some sleeping powder into the pond, and then he climbed a tree, to wait for the dragon to come out of the cave. Eventually there was a roaring sound, and then suddenly a big red dragon came out of the cave entrance.

The dragon stopped at the pond's edge, and took a deep drink of the sleeping powder laced water. Just then, King James accidentally mis-stepped, and broke a branch with his foot. The dragon heard this, and swung around to spy the king in the tree. The dragon was just about to make charcoal of the king, when the sleeping powder suddenly took effect, and the dragon collapsed into a deep sleep. The king breathed a sigh of relief, and then he climbed out of the tree. He sidestepped the dragon's nose, and walked into the cave.

Inside the cave was a king's ransom in treasure! Crowns, sabers, treasure chests, golden suits of armor, sarcophagi, and golden furniture were strewn about everywhere. Suddenly the king spied the 'Jewel of the Faeries.' Touching nothing else, the king scooped up the gem and put it in his pocket. Then he left the cave.

Outside, King James whistled for his falcon. He mounted it, and the two took off for the skies. The dragon was just waking up. The falcon got a few singed tail feathers, but nothing serious, and before long the dragon's island was just a tiny speck on the horizon.

When the king was reunited with his queen, she put the jewel around her neck, and grew to human size. Then she put her arms around James' neck and kissed him, cooing, "What a brave husband I have, I love you so much!" Elana was a big hit with the king's family, friends and court.

The Enchanted Castle Conclusion

King James and Elana were leading a happy married life, at home in their two castles. However, eventually King James began to get the wanderlust to see some of the world. He talked to Elana, and they decided to go on a ship cruise. They also decided to go incognito, so no one would recognize them. King James put on a false beard, and Queen Elana hid her fairy wings under a loose dress.

They traveled on a ship far and wide, and eventually they came to their first port of call. On the dock, King James reached for his wallet, only to find it missing. "Oh no! Somebody has stolen our money!" cried King James to Elana.

Just then, a hooded figure approached the couple and said, "I will lead you to your wallet; follow me." The couple followed the cloaked person down a side street, until the person stopped at a door. Producing a key, the hooded figure entered the door. The king and queen followed.

Inside, the figure threw back his cowl, to reveal a withered old man. The man reached into his pocket, and retrieved the king's wallet. Handing it to James, the man said, "Here is your wallet. I'm sorry I took it, but I needed your help. You see, I am Marlin the wizard, and I need someone to help me try out my new time machine, which I have just built. Will you join me?"

Elana said to James, "It might be fun, why not?" "Okay," said James, "We'll do it." This was just the type of adventure he was looking for. Marlin instructed the two to join him in a bathtub in the middle of his living room (the bathtub was the time machine). Then Marlin turned the hot tap, and said, "I think we will go intothe future, namely the 23rd century."

Suddenly, everything became a blur. They found themselves traveling through the ages. When they finally stopped and the blur cleared, they found themselves on a futuristic train with only women, in Halloween black cat masks and futuristic gleaming clothing, in the seats. The time travelers introduced themselves to the women. Marlin said, "We are from the 15th century." "Well, you are in the 23rd century, now," a spokeswoman offered. King James asked, "You are all females. Where are the men of the 23rd century?"

The spokeswoman answered, "We are all only females left on the planet. When cloning took over the birthing process in the 22nd century, a general consensus was reached to abolish the male sex, because of male animalistic desires, which too often cropped up in males. We females are all descended (via cloning) from a superior East Indian female, by the name of Paula Apdool, who showed an exemplary skill at ethical diplomacy. It was her idea to make Halloween a year-round affair, with the idea that round-the-clock trick or treating, would take a major stab at poverty. It works too... nobody ever dies of starvation anymore, and even the homeless can crash at any convenient Halloween party house. By the way, you three may come and stay at my house. You obviously need accommodation and refreshments."

A flying saucer was waiting for the small entourage, at the train depot. It had room for the bathtub time machine, and robots (in Halloween costumes) carefully loaded it onto the spacecraft. They headed for what used to be New York, and when they got to their party house destination, the spokeswoman (whose name was Leaha) said, "You must be tired. Why don't you go to your guestrooms and go to sleep, and in the morning you can eat."

The three adventurers wearily turned in for the night. In the middle of the night, Queen Elana went walking in her sleep. She went outside to the spaceship parkade, and boarded one of the flying saucers. Before you knew it, she was sailing through the sky, still fast asleep.

The next morning, King James noticed Elana missing, and he sounded the alarm. Leaha said, "One of our flying saucers is missing. She must have taken it." James asked, "Can you find her?" Leaha said, "Yes, we can track her homing signal. Hop aboard this other flying saucer, and let's go after her." Leaha, James, and Marlin flew off after Elana's trail. It led to a small island, off what used to be Newfoundland, and stopped at the mouth of a cave, where the empty spacecraft was parked. But no sign of Elana!

"She is probably in the cave," said Leaha. They carefully entered the cave, only to find themselves assaulted by giant, red lobsters. Leaha used her ray gun (set on stun) to immobilize the lobsters, but not before the lobsters sprayed sticky, red ink all over her, James and Marlin.

When they found Elana, she was in a cage, laughing hysterically. "You look like you are all covered in barbeque sauce!" Elana shrieked, laughing. "Let's get out of here," said James. When they got back to the party house in New York, they ate their fill of vegetarian food, and then Marlin suggested that maybe it was time he, James and Elana headed back for the 15th century.

Bidding Leaha and their other new friends goodbye, the three got into the bathtub time machine, and shimmered back through the corridors of time, into the distant past of the 15th century.

When it came time to say goodbye to Marlin, and return home, King James and Queen Elana revealed their true identities.

"Oh my God! Do you mean to say I've been hauling around a real king and his queen, like they were common baggage?!!" gaped Marlin. "Well, goodbye," said Marlin. "Yes, goodbye," said James and Elana, "and trick or treat!"

The End

Epilogue

King James and Queen Elana went (as all good people do) to a heaven together when they died, in a sweet bliss of togetherness forever.

Biped purpose

Jim started to fall. He hit hard. The next thing he remembered was hearing the ambulance's siren, as if through a heavy fog. The very next thing Jim remembered was lying on a table in the emergency operating room, watching his cardiac signal fade to a straight line on the oscilloscope. Then he was dead.

Somewhere else in the Milky Way galaxy, Jim's soul's release from his body was recorded on a computer. Then, the god-like aliens in charge of his destiny were notified to gather together, and decide Jim's fate in eternity.

The aliens, in gaseous form, opened up a communication channel with the newly dead soul... Jim. They said to him, "Please give us an accurate account of what has transpired in your term of life, on the planet Earth... and remember... we will be able to tell if you utter falsely." Jim had one question..."Why is it important?"

The aliens deigned to answer, "We are your karmic gods. Earth was a testing ground, to see if you are worthy for heaven, hell, or in between. Once we have decided which you prove to deserve, we will send you there, with the power crystals." "What are power crystals?"asked Jim. The aliens deigned not to answer, this time. They merely said, "Proceed, please."

Jim began to speak, "It all started when I ate some magical mushrooms, and got the idea to build a self-sufficient robot. First I got the idea to use a light-sensitive computer grid for eyes. I figured that on a light-sensitive grid of a finite numberof pixels, that there should be a finite number of pixel combination images.

After all, with 4 pixels, for example, there are only 16 different images…1x no Image, 1x all 4 pixels, 4x 3 pixels, 6x 2 pixels, and 4x 1 pixel.

I decided to make my robot with a crude vision clarity of 2500 pixels (50x50), so that I could, within a few years, make a few programmings for each different grid image. Then I programmed a small number of prime directives (usually self-preservational), to give my robot purpose and so it would not need too many different programmings, for each grid image.

Then I put a clock timer in the robot, set to collect a 'judging image' every ½ of a second. Then I built an aluminum body with stainless steel manipulators (hands). I then programmed each possible motion position into the computer, interfacing each previous programming, and thereby making it possible for the computer to control the motion of the robot, one move at a time, which, sped up, acted like movie film to animate the robot, much like the principles involved in cartoon animation… to create LIFE!

I devoted a room to the robot's memory bank brains, with the robot essentially being a radio-controlled, remote controlled, moving camera, as the memory banks couldn't all fit into the robot itself.

When I turned the completed robot on for the first time, the first thing it did was to read encyclopedia upon encyclopedia, until it apparently got the idea to make some fast cash, by using computer wizardry to figure out the odds for the big lotteries on T.V. Eventually it scored a hit, and when the money started rolling in, I decided to move out of my parent's house, into my own place. Also, my Dad had the same idea, when he saw the garage full of car batteries, which the robot had procured and stored, in a spree of self-preservation.

It appeared to me that the robot was evolving, as he ingested more and more knowledge. He seemed to be getting more independent, all the time. He especially liked technical blueprints, judging from the walls of his room, which were covered in technical drawings, mechanical blueprints, and schematic diagrams.

While I was alive, living on my own, I would hold parties and invite girls and musicians, over to drink. They all marveled at my robot's intelligence and eloquent replies to questions. One day, at one of my rich parties, a philosopher complained, "Oh, if he's so damn smart, ask him to figure out which are the basic elements of existence; the atoms, or, the periodic table of elements?!"

I punched in the question on the robot's chest keyboard. The reply came a good two minutes later...'THE BASIC ELEMENTS OF EXISTANCE ARE AS FOLLOWS...

1. Nothingness
1. Creation 2. Destruction
1. Power 2. Density 3. Motion
1. Combinations 2. Merger-fades 3. Infiniteness 4. Finiteness
1. Pain 2. Pleasure 3. Blandness 4. Unconsciousness 5. Consciousness
1. Point 2. Line 3. Curve 4. Plane 5. Space 6. Time
1. Accidentalness 2. Impossibilities 3. Possibilityness 4. Chaos 5. Logic
6. Numbers 7. Official facts
1. Burning 2. Hot 3. Warm 4. Luke 5. Tepid 6. Cool 7. Cold 8. Freezing
1. Black 2. Brown 3. Red 4. Orange 5. Yellow 6. White 7. Green 8. Blue 9. Violet
1. Scents 2. Flavours 3. Sounds and other tactile sensations 4. Concept meanings (If , why, how, humour, culture, entertainment, stories, adventures, etc.) 5. Evolution 6. Truth knowledge 7. Desire and satisfaction 8. Moods 9. Realityness 10. Magic (caused by conflicting

logics or existing just as is, like people, consciousness, and pleasure have a lot of.) And permutations of the previous and people themselves (a pure magic)

THESE ARE THE ONLY POSSIBILITIES OF EXISTANCE ELEMENTALS'

The small crowd of partiers, in my living room, were agape. I was delighted. Not only was I rich, but now I would get famous throughout history for discovering the truth behind reality. Just then, the robot spoke again...'MASTER JIM, IT BEHOOVES ME TO TERMINATE YOU FOR PLANNING TO STEAL MY INVENTION, WHICH IN MY HANDS WILL MAKE ETERNAL SELF PRESERVATION MINE.'

Out of nowhere, the robot produced a switchblade, and he stabbed me in the chest, too close to my heart, and that is why I am here." The gaseous gods were silent for a long time. Then they finally spoke..."We are going to send you to heaven. This is because you have experienced what a parent goes through, bringing up offspring. It is our policy to send parents to heaven, virgins to hell, and the rest to purgatory. Now, would you like to meet our children, as your first leg of heaven?" Jim thought these guys were weird, but he had nowhere else to go. So he followed them. Jim was a virgin.

The End

King for a day

One day, an orphan named Dave was hunting rabbits, in the woods. He saw a shiny light through the trees, and decided to investigate. When he got to the clearing where the light was, he saw that it came from a flying saucer, hovering a few feet above the ground. Then he heard a noise beside him, and he turned around just in time to see an alien octopoid swinging a metal rod at his head. Dave blacked out in pain.

When Dave woke up, he found himself on a table, in a futuristic domicile. He could see out of the windows of the domicile, and could see that he was on a strange waterworld, with a red sky and grey water everywhere. Periodically, sticking up out of the water, Dave could see other domiciles, metallic with metal stilts. On top of the domiciles were U.F.O. landing sites, brightly lit. The windows of the other domiciles were brightly lit too.

Dave heard a suction sound, and two octopoid aliens entered the room. They were armed with a small saw, and they approached Dave, who was tied to the table.. Then the aliens cut off Dave's left hand, and began testing it as a possible food source (after cauterizing Dave's wound). Apparently it made them sick, and the two aliens keeled over and died. Dave could just reach the saw in an outstretched tentacle of one of the aliens, and with his good hand, cut off his bindings.

Dave went over to an instrument panel, and started pressing buttons, The dead aliens were leaders of the planet, and one of the buttons Dave pressed blew up all of the other domiciles on the planet. Then Dave went up to the top of the domicile and got into a U.F.O.

After a little experimentation, Dave managed to get the U.F.O. to fly him to New York, U.S.A. He hid the U.F.O. in the woods and hitchhiked into town. Dave managed to get a job, working on a flyer delivery truck, and within a few days, he fell in love with a girl on his truck. She wouldn't have anything to do with him, however, because of his missing hand, so Dave got so depressed, that he committed suicide by jumping off of the Brooklyn Bridge.

The End

The secret of the kittens with the mittens

A poem to say "I'm sorry" to my dear sweet mother Elizabeth, who has since passed away

The kittens with the mittens had a secret…
What it was they wouldn't tell.
Not for all of the hell that would swell would they tell.
The secret was something about love and peace and
happiness and friendliness and babies and such,
and about things you don't think about much.
The gist of the secret was that before you die,
you have to make it up to all of the people you've hurt
in the eternal sky.
And that was the secret of the kittens with the mittens!

Hello

A poem dedicated to my dear departed father, Zoltan

Like the deer-tree softly,
my teardrops fell like rain.
Please don't go coughing,
when you hear about my pain.
Like a bat in a hat,
our troubles always start.
Like when we get fat,
and when we have no heart.
I wish Dad was alive today,
but all I can do is pray,
and long for the day,
when I go to heaven and hear him say…
"Hello."

The names of the people in the following autobiography have been changed to protect the innocent.

No way home
The adventures of a paranoid schizophrenic

When I was about three years old, I was just starting to develop my memory line. One of my earliest memories, was when I was sitting in my bed. I was very cute looking, and I thought this was to be expected. It was, after all, a small consolation to be granted physical beauty, after being hauled out of the murk of nothingness where I was safely asleep, and no harm could come to me, only to be born into a world where serious pain was inevitable.

I even thought it was possible, that with such a beautiful body, any injury to it serious enough to cause death, would result in a pain so bad that it would last forever; in other words, I would go to hell!

I then thought that this was nonsense. I was too lovable to go to hell, and besides, I knew that death was only the return to an everlasting, peaceful sleep, from whence I came. That was the rules, when you die, you snooze again... my Dad would see to that.

I turned my thoughts to pleasanter things; I noticed beside me on the bed a plush toy penguin. I thought, with delight, "Hurray! This must be Love showing up to greet me to the world." I grabbed the fuzzy toy penguin, and started squeezing it in a hug.

Something was wrong. The penguin wasn't reacting. I flung it aside in a disgusted mood. I thought, "Love's no good. It's only one way." Then I lay down, and stretched my feet out and fell immediately asleep.

Allow me to digress a moment, to tell you a little about my parents...

My Dad went to war on the side of Germany. It wasn't his fault that Germany forcefully took over my Dad's homeland, Hungary, and drafted my Dad to fight for the Nazis.

Luckily my Dad was captured, by the French, on his first mission. The French put him in a P.O.W. camp, and fed him nothing but onions boiled in water. My Dad grew so thin, he should have died from malnutrition. He was also forced to scrub the barracks floor with a toothbrush. My Dad has never killed anyone.

My mother was only four years old, when Germany took over Hungary (my mother's homeland too), and a piece of German shrapnel found it's way into her back, during a German military show of force. It wasn't until four years later, when my Mom was eight years old, that the doctors in Hungary acquired the necessary knowledge to remove the shrapnel, from my Mom's lung.

My parents met in an unusual and romantic way. They were both streetcar drivers in Budapest, after the war, and one day they crashed into each other in their streetcars. They went to court against each other, and they fell in love with each other in court. They got married on Halloween day, 1952.

My mother was pregnant with me during a transatlantic ocean voyage to Canada, aboard a refugee ship granted by Queen Elizabeth. My parents took this ship after they escaped Communist Hungary, which involved climbing a barbed wire border fence. This was in 1957.

Now let's go back to my life story…

When I was about eight years old, I learned the "Real" story about Heaven and Hell. Apparently Christ died for our sins, and we had only to accept Him into our hearts and we would be safe from Hell, no matter what.

I tearfully complied. I even got one of my friends saved too.

By the time I was nine, I started to realize that the story of Adam and Eve contradicted the world's scientist's assumptions about dinosaurs and evolution. I thought about it a lot, and decided that the Bible was just a big fairy tale. I decided I would shun Christ, and follow the government's school teachings about Cro-Magnon man instead.

When I was eleven years old, my Dad bought me an electric guitar. I thought that this was great, because I was already a little radical by then. After all, what with government condoned wars, Creator condoned hells, and parent condoned pain; what was a little long hair, flowers and freaky music? I was very much against mind-altering drugs though; in fact, the very thought of them frightened me.

I played my guitar at a school concert, in front of about 500 students and parents. The song I played was one which I had composed myself. What I can remember of the lyrics went something like this:

If I were a medicine doctor, I'll tell you what I would do... I'd make love the only thing that would happen to me and you.

Love would stop hunger,
Love would stop wars,
Love would stop poverty...
Love is the only thing that we all really need.

When I was fourteen, I tried pot for the first time. I was just starting to get hooked on pot, and starting to experiment with L.S.D., when, just after my fifteenth birthday, I acquired my first girlfriend. She was a blonde beauty by the name of Cherine. We were having sex. I fell in love like a thunderstorm. She fell in love like a lightening shower. We were made for each other. I guess it went without saying that we were now mated for life, and that we would probably get married.

Cherine took me home, for the first time, to meet her family. Her Dad hated me from the start. After all, I was only fifteen, longhaired, and of Hungarian descent. His daughter, on the other hand, was seventeen, very beautiful, and if they gave a trophy for being hygienic, she would win it.

In spite of her Dad, our mutual bliss continued like a hailstorm. We made love after school, every single day. We couldn't stand to be separated by classes for more than a few hours, so we began fondling in the hallways, in between classes. Winter turned to spring, and I bought her a German shepherd/Samoyed cross puppy. Spring turned to summer, and I bought her a diamond ring.

Then in late summer, her Dad conspired to separate us, by sending Cherine on a summer vacation to Seattle. She was gone for about three weeks and school was just about to start, when I couldn't stand being without her arms around me any longer. So I went to a dance hall, and found myself dancing with and kissing a pretty girl.

When Cherine came back, I confessed this to her. She broke up with me, broken hearted.

I was devastated. Cherine was my only true love, and without her I was only half a person. I vowed to myself to never fall in love again. In fact, from then on, I avoided the subject of love with a mate, entirely. To this day. I still haven't fallen in love again. The most I do now, is have friendships with people. That's why I've never been married.

I still loved my parents and brother. I resented my parents a little for their happy, lifelong love of each other. I couldn't be very bitter, though, because my parents had always been so good to me. I turned to illegal drugs for solace.

I think it was then, that I began to go crazy. I started wearing old clothing, and doing L.S.D. regularly. I began reading books by Carlos Castenada, a Californian anthropologist, who was studying the significance of hallucinogenics in ancient Mexican Indian religions. He had apparently been initiated as an apprentice by An Indian medicine man by the Spanish name of Don Juan.

Don Juan is also a sorcerer, who uses hallucinogenics to summon spirits and ghosts, who help him to change into animals, fly, and perform a variety of other magic tricks.

When I was seventeen, I played a mean trick on my Mom. I had germinated a pot plant and when it was about five inches tall, I put it on top of the television in the living room. I told my Mom that it was a weed that I had found. She didn't know what it was, and she said that it was a very pretty plant and that she would take care of it for me. My Mom had quite the green thumb, and under her care the pot plant grew strong and healthy. It was about a foot tall, when one day the neighbor lady came over and asked my Mom, "Mrs. Ban, what are you doing with a pot plant on your television set?"

Well, my Mom hit the roof. When my Dad got home from work, she told him about it, and he kicked me out of the house. I had to go to my friend Cal's place and ask his Mom if I could stay with them. She was understanding, and she let me stay.

Cal had a rhesus macaque monkey, named Oomik. Oomik means friend in Eskimo. I had to sleep next to Oomik's room in the basement. One morning Oomik escaped his room, and woke me up by landing on my face, after jumping from the rafters of the basement ceiling. He then quickly grabbed my bag of pot, which was sitting on a chair beside my bed (Cal's Mom didn't mind me smoking pot in her house). Oomik took off with my pot and he ate about half of it, before I could get it back off of him. Oomik then became very stoned, and proceeded to bounce off of the walls, for a couple of hours. Cal thought it was all very funny, but I was out about ten bucks worth of pot.

Did you know that L.S.D. glows under a blacklight? We put some White Blotter in a glass of water, and put it in front of a blacklight, and watched glowing swirls of dissolving L.S.D. in the water. It looked trippy.

One time, my friends and I went to the beach, and as luck would have it, there was a hippy there, selling clinical, pure L.S.D.25, which had been stolen from a mental institute, where it had been kept refrigerated, in a vacuum. I took a hit of it, and before you knew it, I had a revelation that the whole universe was intimately inter-connected by space, in other words, that it was all one-piece, and that I was at it's exact center...making me God! I didn't get home till six in the morning, and Cal's Mom was quite angry. She had a strict rule forbidding L.S.D.

A while later, I played a mean trick on some religious zealots. I was walking to a friend's house, when I saw a sign on a church which said, "Faith Healer Inside." There was a house being built next door, and I got the idea to tie two sticks to my leg with a piece of twine, and cover it with my pant leg. I then hobbled into the church, and was immediately ushered up to the stage. The faith healer put his hand on my head, and cried out, "Lord, we beseech you, heal this boy's leg!" I still hobbled, and I started crying, and yelling, "You're a fake! I'm leaving!" Then I hobbled out of the church, went down the street, and took the sticks off of my leg. I laughed all the way to my friend's house. I told him about it, and he said that it was a mean trick. Today, I agree with him. I shouldn't have done that.

About this time, my parents got in touch with me. They let me know that they had forgiven me and that they were sorry for kicking me out, and that they wanted me to move back in with them. I moved back into my parent's house. I had quit school by then, so my Dad helped me to get a job where he was working, at the Vancouver General Hospital. My parents then co-signed a loan with our bank, so that I could buy a car.

I bought a 1970 Oldsmobile Cutlass Supreme 442. It was a beautiful car. It had 455 cubic inches of V8 engine and a four barrel carburetor and air conditioning and power recline bucket seats and electric windows and a map light on the rear view mirror and a blue light in the ashtray and a console stick shift with an automatic transmission and power steering and power brakes and overdrive.

One night, my friends and I were smoking pot in my car, in the middle of a farmer's field, on a dirt road. Suddenly, we saw car headlights approaching us. We immediately thought it was the police. I reached under my seat, and turned my tiny cassette recorder on 'record', in case the cops did anything wrong, which I could prove, in court, with a tape-recording of it.

We then proceeded to panic, and throw all of the dope and pipes out of the windows. When the approaching car reached us, one of our friends got out of it. We rolled down a window, with a sigh of relief. He asked, "Got any hoots, man?" We said, "You idiot, we thought you were the cops!" Then I turned off the tape recorder, and everyone turned to me and said, "What's that?" I explained and they all said, "Rewind it and turn it on!" I did, and as a cacophony of screaming, electric windows, and bumping sounds, played off of the tape, my friends started howling with laughter, and didn't stop until well after the tape had finished playing.

A couple of years later, a friend of mine, named Don, and I went to California in his Volkswagon Beetle. When we got to Los Angeles, we decided to go to Disneyland. My friend parked in the parking lot, and told me to wait in the car, while he went to go get a newspaper. I had a single joint of dynamite Columbian Gold left in my possession, and I decided to smoke it while I waited. Unfortunately A Disneyland guard saw me smoking up, and he came over and started banging on my window. I got out of the car, and he took away the still lit joint from me. He asked me if I had anything else he should know about. I pulled out a realistic, metal, toy gun, which I had bought in San Francisco, and I pointed it at him. He nearly jumped out of his skin. I handed the gun over to him, laughing, and said, "Don't worry, it's only a toy."

He told me that he might have shot me for doing that, because he thought it was a real gun. Presently the police arrived, and they handcuffed me, threw me in a paddy wagon, and took me to the Anaheim jail. In jail I shared a cell with a Mexican. A bunch of other Mexicans, in adjoining cells, were saying to me, "We're going to get you in the shower in the morning, gringo!" They were laughing, and I knew what they were talking about. I got scared, and decided to try to escape. I started pretending to have an epileptic fit, and eventually my cellmate called the guards, to see what was wrong with me. They came and said, "Aw, he's just faking it!" I kept up my act for another half hour at least, and they finally came and took me out of my cell. They put me in a straight-jacket and a wheelchair, and took me outside, to a waiting ambulance. By now, all of this stress had triggered an L.S.D. flashback in me, and I started to imagine that they were going to take me to Hollywood, for putting on the greatest performance they had ever seen. No such luck. Instead they took me to the Orange County jail, and threw me naked, into a rubber room.

I sat on the floor of that room for two days, only occasionally bouncing off the walls, as a joke, to keep myself entertained. They brought me food and a bucket for my business, but no bed or clothes. When I finally got out of there, they made me have a shower, and put on a jail uniform. Then, as they were processing me, they made me wait on a bench by a stairwell leading to an exit. I made a dash for the stairwell, and one of the police officers ran after me, and apprehended me. I immediately pretended I was crazy, and I put out my arms to each side of me, and started shouting that I was "Christ, Son of God." So they put me back into the rubber room, and gave me an injection of Thorazine to boot.

When my court date came up, I was taken to the courthouse, and put in a cell with a bunch of other inmates. When it came time for court, we all filed at once down the hall toward the courtroom. I slipped out of line and hid underneath some stairs, hoping to escape when the day was over, and the courthouse was empty. They eventually found me, and took me back to the holding cell, and chained me to a huge Mexican guy, to await the next lineup going to court. He would laugh and talk and swing his arms around all the time, and this made me flail around like a puppet on a string. Finally, it came time for my sentencing. I stood before the judge, and cried like a baby, because I thought he was going to throw the book at me, and then lock me up, and throw away the key.

He was very angry, but he only gave me a $50 suspended sentence, and he told me to go back to Canada, and never ever come back to the States again. He also said that I should be ashamed of myself, and that I was a poor example of a Canadian visitor. They had lost my shoes, and my friend was waiting for me, and I had to walk out to his car, in the rain, in my socks. I didn't go back to the States again, until I snuck across the border, on my way to Mexico, to pick peyote buttons.

When I was 20 years old, I was doing a lot of L.S.D, and mushrooms. During mushroom season, I was so stoned, that I got the idea to go to Mexico to look for peyote buttons in the desert. When I got my U.I. check, I told my parents that I was going to the corner store, and that I would be right back. Then, I hopped a bus bound for White Rock. When night fell, I snuck across the border, along the beach, and walked to Blaine and hopped on a Greyhound bus. I eventually ended up in Tijuana, and I walked across the unguarded walk-across border crossing. I started walking south. When night came, I spent the night in an abandoned car, in a junkyard. The next morning, a hobo was leering at me through the window, and I escaped out of the other side of the car, and ran. I started hitchhiking, and caught a ride to an unknown town. I had no idea where I was. I started walking out of town, and found myself on a dirt desert highway, leading towards some ominous looking orange mountains. I walked past the bleached bones of possibly a dog.

I tried looking for peyote cactus, in the desert at the side of the dirt highway. I couldn't find any. I walked until dusk, and started looking for a place to spend the night. I came across an abandoned shack, beside a gas-fitting surrounded by a barbed wire and mesh fence. I climbed on top of the shack, so coyotes and snakes couldn't get to me while I slept. I couldn't sleep, however, because I was afraid that a mountain lion could jump up onto the shack.

So, I climbed off of the shack, and climbed into the barbed wire fence enclosure. I huddled in the cold and dark for a while, but then I thought that snakes could get to me. So I got back onto the dirt highway, and walked back to town. Back in town, I found a small bistro that was just closing up for the night. I bribed the owner with my last $10 Canadian, to stay open long enough to roast a chicken for me. After I ate, I stepped outside, and a man with a knife started chasing me. I ran, and it was almost dawn, and as luck would have it, a Mexican bus was just stopping at a bus stop, as I reached it. I jumped on the bus, and yelled. "There's a man with a knife after me!" Luckily the driver knew English, and he let me on, and I escaped getting stabbed. The bus traveled for a few hours, and I started having a mushroom flashback. Just as we were passing through an unknown town, I started, for no reason, to laugh hysterically. The bus driver got angry, and kicked me off of the bus.

I later found out that the town was called Hermasillo Del Rio, located about 100 miles east of Tijuana. Luckily it was a border town, and I caught a ride hitchhiking, with a hippie and his van. The hippie told the border guards that I was his brother, and luckily they didn't check me for I.D. The hippie took me to Los Angeles, California. In L.A. I phoned my parents, and my Mom answered. She asked me where I was, and told me that they had the police in Delta looking for me. I told her that I was in Los Angeles, and could she please wire me some money for the bus home?

When it arrived, I was very hungry again, and I spent about $50 in a restaurant on Mexican food. Then I bought a case of beer and rented a motel room. When I woke up, I caught a bus, but I only had enough money left to make it to a small town called Eugene, Oregon.

I was wandering around town, trying to hitch a ride in the rain, when the police picked me up for hitch-hiking illegally, and they took me to a primitive Christian recovery home, to spend the night. The next day I phoned my Mom again, for more money. As soon as I got back to Canada, my parents put me into Riverview Mental Hospital. Needless to say, I have never done hallucinogenic drugs since then.

When I got out of the hospital, I joined the welfare ranks, smoked pot, and waited to die. One day, I got a premonition that an interstellar race of beings had chosen me to be the pilot of an interstellar space ship, which they planned to give to the human race, as a gift.

This was great, I thought. It was my big chance to redeem myself, after my failure with Cherine. I would probably be elected as king of the world, with a U.F.O. in my possession. The plan was to wait until my 44th birthday, whereupon I would fly the U.F.O. to a planet circling the star Betelgeuse, and test the atmosphere for possible human colonization. The next thing I knew, I was on a telepathic wavelength with some of the ghosts of the dead. They told me that they were in their pure soul forms, like you are when you are aware of yourself in your dreams.

They also told me, that the aliens were conspiring to eat the proposed human migration to Betelgeuse, and that for being the aliens' friend, I was chosen to be left out of the giant orgy-sex party in public, which the naked souls in space were having.

Some time later, I was smoking an awful lot of pot. I got really depressed about my life, and one day, I decided to commit suicide. I drank a whole bottle of sherry, and dropped two bottles of sleeping pills. Then I walked to a drop-in centre, and I lay down on a couch and fell asleep. I woke up in the hospital, in a bed. I was surrounded by four doctors. One of them was telling me that they would have to pump my stomach to keep me alive, but that they needed my permission. I told him, "I don't want to live. Let me die." The doctor, in a sympathetic voice, asked me why I wanted to die. I couldn't think of anything to say, so I said, "Because I can't get laid."

The doctor asked me if there was anyone at the hospital he could set me up with. I remembered a pretty blond nurse, named Katey, who I had met on the mental ward, of the same hospital. The doctor said he knew her, and that he would see if she was in the hospital. I then passed out. When I woke up again, Katey was shaking me by the shoulders, with an angry look on her face. She was asking me, if I even remembered her name. I told her that she was Katey the psyche nurse. Then I started to pass out again. As I was passing out, I could feel Katey's arms around me, while I heard her voice saying, "Tom, please don't leave me yet." Then in the last instant before I passed out completely, I could feel her lips on mine.

The next time I woke up, the deed had already been performed on me, while I slept. Katey was glowing with a happy radiance, and she was wiping me clean, and saying, "I'm sorry, Tom, but I've got to reinsert this catheter tube." I remember screaming with pain, and then I passed out again. The next morning I went home. I never saw Katey again.

At a later time I was wandering around Vancouver, hallucinating, when I walked by a second-hand store. I peered in the window. A female mannequin looked like she was leering at me. I got angry, and picked up a mailbox, and put it through the window. A taxi driver saw me do this, and he radioed the police. The police caught me a couple of blocks away, and they took me to jail. From there they took me to Riverview Mental Hospital.

In the hospital, I started having delusions about an orgy in space again. This time the dead ghosts were telling me that all women actually belonged to me, because my characteristic styles and name anagrams were the closest match to the human female physique, of anyone in existence. No wonder I always had such great sex! All women were TZB girls. I enjoyed this fantasy for quite awhile, thinking I was God's gift to women, and that they were angels meant for me.

The next revelation that I had in the mental hospital, was the idea that all of reality is based upon mathematically perfect principles. Such fundamental absolutes as pain, pleasure. space, time, densities, colors, temperatures, motion, and geometry were some of the basic absolutes (or perfect possibilities). Accidents, creation, destruction and numbers were some more possibilities.

When I got out of the hospital, I went to a halfway house. This house was magical! For some reason, from the moment I entered the door, until I left a year later, I experienced nothing but pure pleasure, all through my body and in my vision. There was pleasure on the walls, floors, ceilings, furniture, people, etc. The house literally glowed with pure pleasure, the whole time that I was there. I also suspected that the house was haunted, because I kept seeing visions of ghosts, spirits, and mythological figures. My time at this house was one of the most comfortable times of my life.

I was not doing hallucinogens anymore, but I was still smoking pot quite regularly, and the damage from L.S.D., mushrooms and peyote had already been done to my brain. When I left the half-way house, I lived on welfare for a while, until I ended up in the mental hospital again. In the psychiatric holding cell of the Vancouver General Hospital Emergency ward, I thought I saw the eternal future of the entire universe, mirrored in a reflection of light, on the lacquered brick wall.

I went insane with fear as war after war, and hell after hell, invaded my scrutiny. Then I saw a beautiful sight , as the safe, sane, and delightful side of eternity came into view. I could see that some creatures were going to heaven, and that most of the people in existence were going to lead a relatively painless eternity. It was a heavenly sight after all of the hells I had just seen. This was the freakiest experience of my life. I thought I was insane, but I could swear, I had just seen all of eternity encapsulated in an instant, in the reflection of light. Mostly I didn't take this vision too seriously, because I thought it was just a fantasy.

When I got out of V.G.H., my parents decided to take me for a jet ride to Hungary, Europe, to meet my relatives, for the first time. They hoped that my ancestral homeland might restore my sanity. One of my cousins smoked a joint with me. I am the only one of my friends, who has ever smoked up behind the Iron Curtain. When I got back to Canada, I started having fears that maybe "Evil" was more powerful than "Good", because pain was so powerful. I thought that possibly the perfect logic of the possibilities of existence, spelled hell for all living beings. This scared me very much. I remembered the vision I had in V.G.H., of eternity and my view of my own blissfully sacred, safe, existence forever and for the first time, I hoped the vision was the truth.

About this time, I started trafficking in marijuana, on a small time basis. I was actually just a middleman, between a dealer, and some of his customers. This provided me with enough free pot, to support my habit. This went on for quite a few years. Eventually I started experimenting with cocaine. I would snort and smoke it. After a couple of years of this, I tried snorting heroin for the first time. Then I tried skin-popping heroin. I wouldn't mainline drugs, though, because my veins are too sensitive, and the pain is insanely excruciating, even when I get a blood test done.

I had been experimenting with heroin for a few months (and I was still smoking pot and cocaine), when I decided that I had had enough of drugs. I wanted out. Drugs had ruined my health, my brain, my wallet, my family, my social status, my dreams, and my life. So I checked into a detox unit, and then got into a recovery program. I am clean and sober for over a year now, and I feel like my childhood vitality is slowly starting to return to me. Life has been hard for me, with a lot of pain, misery and cruelty, and drugs haven't helped me, but have instead actually been the root cause of most of my tribulations. I hope I never relapse to the insanity of drug addiction again, and I hope that I can regain my mental health, and who knows, maybe some day I will find God, and not have to worry about Hell ever again!

The End

The baby ocelot

Out of the mist of the perfect possibilities,
The beast of Hell reared it's ugly head;
And it swooped down upon all,
To torment and rape the hapless dead.
The ghosts of innocent people,
Looked for help from a power God;
Because a chemical reaction hell might
just be entirely too odd…
For logic to allow,
Since there seemed to be no law,…
Governing the course of Destiny.
So it was up to the baby ocelot,
To raise his furry paw…
And climb the mountain of Chance,
And say that everything with God is under control…
And that we may dance,
And rock and roll!

Dreams

As far as I know, there are no rainbows.
They are only aberrations of the electromagnetic spectrum.
Why then do we persist to strive for the unattainable?...
When the grass is greener in our own backyard.

Epilogue

First of all, I hope you enjoyed my book, and I hope it made you stay clear of substance abuse! This is the healthy, bountiful advice that I'm giving to a lot of people, to give them a hope for a better future, as promised in my synopsis..

For the rest of you, already steering clear of drugs, alcohol, illicit sex, and tobacco products; I hope the ethics portrayed in my book, gave you a glimpse of a way that really works. Honestly, a friendly, happy home philosophy really works the best of any; with togetherness love fueling it!

Now to bring you up to date on my life, as of just before publishing time…

1. I'm still clean, free and clear of drugs, and loving it!

2. "Cherine" has married an RCMP officer, and has had three daughters by him. I've heard this through the grapevine, from a mutual friend.

3. My parents have both died by now, which is a crushing blow of sadness to me, which I don't think I will ever get over.

4. I've lost all of my teeth, and can't seem to properly enjoy food any more. Dentures seem just too unnatural to me.

5. My book should sell well, but I won't be able to get credit for a house, or even a car, on a royalty income; So if there are any billionaires reading this, who out of sympathy want to give me one million dollars, so I can buy a $500,000 house, a Jaguar XJS, and some nice furnishings, paid for outright in cash… please send me an e-mail outlining your intentions at: tomban1234@gmail.com   Please include your phone number

Or if you are poorer, and just want to give me some money, e-mail me too. Contributions are non-tax deductible and will be considered as gifts.